Charles M. Schulz

It's Baseball Season, Again!

HarperHorizon

An Imprint of HarperCollinsPublishers

First published in 1999 by HarperCollins*Publishers* Inc.
http://www.harpercollins.com

http://www.snoopy.com
ISBN 0-06-107550-7
Printed in China

"Where's my baseball glove? It's almost baseball time again . . ."

"Has anyone seen my glove?"

I hope he's forgotten he hung me in the closet . . . Please don't look in the closet . . . It's embarrassing to be the glove for the kid who's never won a game . . .

"And my baseball cap . . . has anyone seen my cap?"

Shh! Don't tell him I'm here under the coat . . .

"All right, gang, it's time to start our spring training! I don't want to hear any more complaining about a little snow on the ground! Where's our shortstop?"

"This is spring training! We need the practice, don't we?"

"Hey! Where's everybody going?! What about spring training?!! Come back! This is only a little storm! Come back!!"

"Hey, manager . . . I think your dog
is afraid of thunder."

"Hey! Where is everybody going? Come back! It's going to clear up! The sun is breaking through!"

"Sorry, I thought it was the sun . . ."

"All right, I don't have to remind you how important this game is today ..."

"I'm glad you're not like some baseball managers, Charlie Brown. I read about one manager who used to get real mad at his players ... If a player did something dumb, the manager would pull the player's cap down over his head ..."

"I shouldn't have mentioned it ..."

"This was a good suggestion . . . If a player makes a dumb mistake, I pull his cap down over his head . . ."

"That's for swinging at a pitch that was six feet over your head!"

"Two hundred and seven to nothing!
We have the worst team in the history
of baseball!"

"I wish I could talk with the man
who invented baseball ..."

"To get his advice?"